CINNAMON
A HORSE FORCED INTO THE SEX TRADE

CINNAMON IS A SPECIAL HORSE

HE'S ALWAYS HAPPY TO RUN. OF COURSE

CINNAMON WINS ALL THE RACES

HE PUTS SMILES ON PEOPLE'S FACES

CINNAMON HAS A GOOD CAREER

RETIREMENT WILL SOON BE NEAR

UNTIL CINNAMON BROKE HIS LEG

AND NOW HE WILL BE FORCED TO PEG

LADY HORSES ALL DAY LONG

CINNAMON WILL BE USED FOR HIS DONG

AS HE GETS READY FOR HIS DAILY JERK

HE REALIZES. THAT THIS IS SEX WORK.

ONCE HE WAS THE STAR OF THE SHOW

CINNAMON HAS BECOME A HO

If you want to reach me.

TW: @bradgosse
IG: @bradgosse
FB: @bradgosse
TIKTOK: @bradgosse
Youtube: @BradGosse

If you want clipart from this book.
@vectortoons
VectorToons.com

THE END. WRITTEN BY BRAD GOSSE

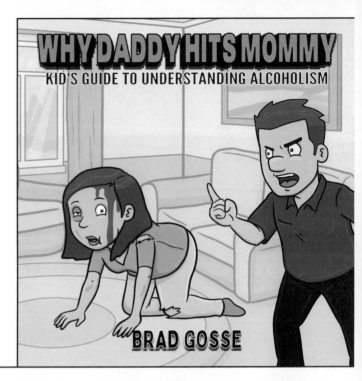

CHECK OUT MY OTHER BOOKS AVAILABLE NOW

CHECK OUT MY OTHER BOOKS AVAILABLE NOW

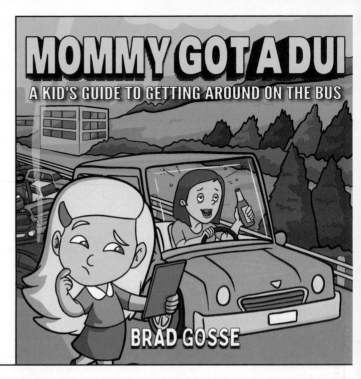

CHECK OUT MY OTHER BOOKS AVAILABLE NOW

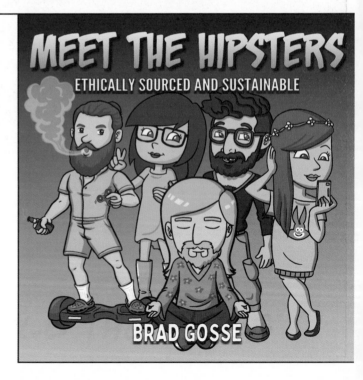

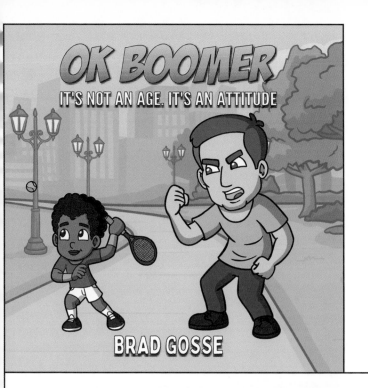

CHECK OUT MY OTHER BOOKS AVAILABLE NOW

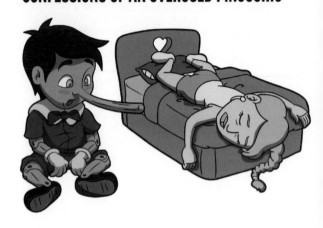

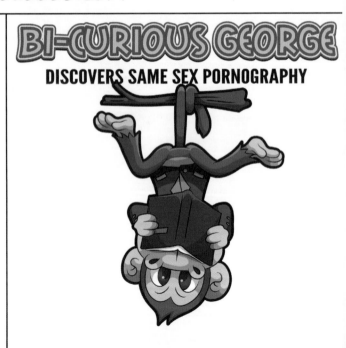

Printed in Great Britain
by Amazon

12484265R00016